The Little Blue and the Christmas Tree

by Harriet Tuppen

illustrated by Branislav Gapic

To get FREE printable coloring pages
of Little Blue and his friends, visit:

www.tuppenbooks.com/freebies/

ISBN-13: 978-1519308474
ISBN-10: 1519308477

For Noah

It was nearly Christmas in Builders Town! Little Blue was playing in the snow with his friends.

Even Big Yellow was in a good mood! "Back to work, everyone!" he laughed. "Once we've finished, we can go and choose our Christmas tree."

Hurray! The team worked hard and soon everything was finished. They set out cheerfully through the snow to the Christmas tree farm.

They found the
perfect tree in
no time.

Big Yellow heaved it into the air and dropped it gently onto Wide Red's back.

Then the friends drove proudly
back to the construction site.

But Tall Orange was so excited that she rushed and slipped, crane over tracks.

CRASH!

SMASH!

TINKLE!

The decorations were ruined!
And everyone was unhappy with
Tall Orange. She felt terrible.

Then Little
Blue had
an idea.

He could see lots of things lying around that would look great on the Christmas tree.

Soon the friends were busy making
a pile of new decorations. But Tall
Orange was too sad to join in.

When everyone started
to decorate the tree,
Tall Orange sat by
herself.

Then Little Blue stopped. "Friends are more important than pretty decorations," he said. "Tall Orange, will you please put the star up?"

Tall Orange came
shyly forward and
took the star from
Little Blue.

She lifted it ever so carefully to the top of the tree. Everyone cheered!

Later on, the friends stood side by side in the moonlight. They all agreed that this was the best Christmas tree they had ever built. Especially Tall Orange!

The End

Printed in Great Britain
by Amazon.co.uk, Ltd.,
Marston Gate.